D0839362

Short and Sweet

Short and Sweet

13 sweet, romantic stories

By Susan Page Davis

Tea Tin Press
Dexter, Kentucky

Contents

A Piece of Cake

I knew he was the one when the cake went out the window.

Nick was a writer at the magazine where I managed the office, and we had been working together for a year. At first, I didn't think I liked him.

True, he was smart and witty, but he was almost too clever. I told him last spring the editor would hate his article on edible soap, but Nick didn't believe me. That piece went to recycling. But I didn't think he'd like the one about working vacations, either, and I was wrong.

It was a great hit, and we got about a ton and a half of reader mail on the piece.

Even before Nick was hired, I admired his writing. He wrote features for a metropolitan newspaper's Sunday section then, and everyone at our magazine felt we were fortunate to get him for our team. But I'm not one to gush over good-looking bachelors. I left that to the clerks and interns in the office.

Still, Nick was always friendly, and we kept up a lively banter whenever our paths crossed. After a few months I realized the tone was morphing into a mild flirtation. I told myself Nick was that way with all the women, but after a while I began to think of him as more than a coworker. A friend... and possibly more.

It reached the point where I realized Nick wanted to move into second gear, but I wasn't sure that I was ready. My studied professionalism warred with his unpredictable kookiness, and after all, I'd gotten used to living alone and spending most of my free time alone. Did I really want to disrupt my orderly life? Because there was no question, Nick would be a major disruption.

Then our editor retired. His hand-picked successor, Parker Ryback, would take over on September first. I made it my business to learn everything about the new boss. Ryback was coming to us after three years as editor of *Howland's*, a high-profile lifestyle magazine.

As the day of his arrival drew closer, I went into a list-making, party-planning frenzy. He would walk off the elevator and into a celebration befitting our new managing editor.

Nick thought I went a little overboard. "How do you know he's not death on office parties?"

I smiled with a bit of smugness. "Last year *Howland's* had a Christmas party our people would envy. Mr. Ryback presided, and a good time was had by all."

"Ah."

That's all Nick said—"Ah." He didn't even ask how I knew this, giving me a chance to show off my sneaky research capabilities. It made me furious… but not furious enough to make me abandon my list.

"Cake, welcome banner, paper plates, printed napkins…"

"You're loony," Nick muttered, ambling toward his desk.

On September first all was in place. The office was tastefully festooned with blue and gold streamers, a bunch of balloons, and the banner. I had laid out the refreshments precisely on the table in the conference room, with the cake as the centerpiece. It was a work of art, with rows of frosting roses. Perfect Arial letters piped in blue frosting read:

WELCOME
MR. RYBACK

Nick stood at my elbow, looking critically at the confection.

"What?" I asked.

"Nothing."

"There's always something."

"Hm."

"Would you quit it?" I'd had enough with his hms and ahs. "Mr. Ryback is a sociable person. He'll feel welcome, part of the team."

"Is this a play to keep him from reorganizing his staff?"

"How can you say that? We're a terrific staff. He wouldn't dare replace anyone in this office with some tagalong from *Howland's*."

"Hm."

I elbowed him.

"Ouch!"

"You're so pessimistic."

Nick glared back. "You're so naïve."

Just then Jennifer, one of the clerks, poked her head in at the door of the conference room.

"Mr. Ryback's not coming today."

"What?" I felt lightheaded.

"Sorry. His father died. He may not be in until next week. We're supposed to work on the February issue layout."

I sighed in defeat. "All this work for nothing."

"You could freeze the cake," Nick said.

"Are you nuts? Feed the new boss frozen cake next week?"

"Well, then…" He looked at the cake and arched his eyebrows in the silly, endearing look that made me want to hug

12

him or strangle him, I wasn't sure which.

"Sure, why not?"

Nick grinned and yelled to the office at large, "No boss today, but we've got cake!"

Within ten minutes, the place was in chaos. *So much for the February layout,* I thought.

Nick brought me a slice of cake on a paper plate, and my personal mug. "Green tea." He held it out like a peace offering.

I gave him a grudging smile and accepted the mug. "Thanks. I think I'll take the afternoon off, after I clean up this mess."

"What? The queen of efficiency leaving early? You never leave early."

I smiled and sat down hard in my chair. A little too hard, as tea slopped onto my challis skirt.

"I'll get you a napkin."

I almost yelled, "No, save the printed napkins!" But then I realized I wasn't going through this again. Whenever Mr. Ryback made his debut, I would greet him calmly and brief him on the latest developments, just as I used to with the old boss. Businesslike. Practical. No streamers.

I followed Nick to the conference room. The cake was half gone. Now it said:

COME
BACK

Nick smiled wryly. "Anyone would think it's a bon voyage party." He handed me a napkin, but it was too late for my skirt.

I sighed wearily. Tears were threatening to sabotage me, and I realized how much the welcome party had meant to me.

"Are you okay?" Nick asked.

I nodded miserably.

"I'll tell the guys to get down to work," he said. "A half hour of mayhem won't ruin the day."

"That's true. Letting off steam once in awhile is good. We can still get a lot accomplished today."

"Right." He eyed me cautiously, and I managed a wobbly smile.

It's not so very wild, I thought. Just cake, lemonade, and a little horseplay. We stepped out of the conference room.

Jennifer caught my eye. She was on the phone at her desk, and her expression was more panic than party. She waved at me frantically.

I pushed Nick aside and strode to Jennifer's desk. She stared at me, her green eyes wide with shock as she replaced the receiver.

"Mr. Ryback is coming after all."

"Today?"

"Yes. He decided to put in an appearance, since we were expecting him."

I gulped. "Very thoughtful. How long do we have?"

"He's downstairs."

I stared stupidly at Nick.

"Sixty seconds," Nick said.

We went into action. The clerks pulled down the streamers and stuffed them discreetly into wastebaskets, hiding them under scrap paper. Jennifer whisked away the debris. Everyone stuck plates of cake in desk drawers and jettisoned paper cups. The art editor crammed the balloons into the storage closet, trying unsuccessfully to shut the door on them. Nick strategically popped a few with a letter opener so the door would close.

"The cake!" I whispered. The elevator doors were opening down the hall.

Nick grabbed the tray and headed for the window over the parking lot. I ran ahead of him and opened it. Two floors below us was the closed dumpster. The postman was about to enter the building, and Nick seized the opportunity.

"Hey!" he yelled.

The postman craned his neck to look up, his mouth open. "Yeah?"

"Open the dumpster!" Nick's urgent request was carefully modulated, so no one inside the office could hear it.

The remains of the cake flew out, and I slid into my chair just as the office door opened and Mr. Ryback entered, smiling mournfully.

"Good morning, people."

I jumped up to greet him as Nick gently closed the window.

"Good morning, sir," I said. "I'm so sorry about your father. It was good of you to come."

I introduced him to everyone in the office. Nick was one step ahead of me, signaling a typist to wipe the smear of frosting from her cheek and kicking a crumpled napkin under the copier. In spite of the chaos inside me, I managed to stay outwardly calm and show Mr. Ryback to his new private office.

When I returned to my desk twenty minutes later, there was a yellow sticky note on my monitor.

Great job, Melissa. But I know you— you won't really take the afternoon off. How about dinner instead? I promise, no cake. Nick

I looked across the room. He was watching me, his eyebrows raised in anticipation. I nodded slowly, and he smiled.

The End

Where There's Smoke...

"You've got a group of fourth-graders coming at ten this morning," Polly said.

"Great. I love that age." Julie tied on her long skirt over her shorts and adjusted the gathered mobcap she wore each day.

"Well, just a heads-up." Polly straightened the fold of Julie's shawl across her shoulder. "You may be evaluated during your presentation."

Julie swallowed hard. "Already? I've

only been doing this for three weeks. I was hoping to get a little more comfortable before something like this came up."

"Yes, well, the museum's personnel director says it's time. Get your cooking fire burning, and I'll see you later." Polly turned in a swirl of woolen skirts and linen petticoats and left the room.

Julie went to the fireplace and began methodically laying the fire. It would take an hour and a half for the wood to burn down into the pile of glowing red coals she needed. When the students came to bake a cake on the hearth with her, she wanted everything to be perfect.

She loved her new job as a historical interpreter at the museum, and she hoped to keep it for a long time. Even working in a sweltering colonial kitchen in the middle of summer would be worth it.

She checked all her cooking utensils

and ingredients and laid a stack of handouts with period recipes on the long pine table that was her work surface.

Promptly at ten, a group of fifteen energetic nine-year-olds burst into her kitchen. Two middle-aged women quieted them and brought a measure of order.

"Greetings," Julie said with her brightest smile. "Prithee be seated. It gives me great pleasure to have so many helpers this day."

She launched into her routine, showing the children the odd tools and kettles that had become her familiar friends, and then demonstrated the balance scale.

"Now, who will come and weigh out a pound of flour for me?"

As she scanned the group, she noticed a somber man leaning against the doorjamb, watching her with brooding dark eyes. Her heart lurched. The director had arrived.

She swallowed hard. If he wasn't one of her bosses, she could throw him a cheerful greeting and include him in the activity. He was very attractive when it came down to it, but his watchful brown eyes kept her on edge.

She realized her smile had slipped, and quickly put it back in place, reaching out to a freckle-faced little boy. He was obviously one of the class's mischief-makers, and Julie pulled his name off the tag he wore on his striped T-shirt.

"Ben."

"Yeah?" His eyes gleamed with anticipation.

"Would you be kind enough to assist me, lad?"

She went on with the demonstration, calling on each of the children in turn to perform a simple task. One broke the eggs into a pottery bowl, two carefully measured her spices and sugar, and another beat the batter for her. Ben slopped the flour all over the tabletop, and a gawky little girl dropped one of the eggs on the floor. Julie managed to keep her smile intact and assured the children that it was all part of learning to cook on the hearth. Through it all, the handsome man observed her from his post in the doorway.

She thought she saw his lips twitch when she knocked the poker over and it clattered to the slate hearth. Or maybe it was a grimace. Julie wiped her hands on her apron and cleared her throat.

"All right, children, now is the time to pull the coals out onto the hearth, where we'll bake our cake."

Carefully she herded the red-hot embers into a pile before the fireplace and settled the Dutch oven on it.

"What do we do next?"

Fifteen eager hands flew up.

"Katelyn?" she prompted the smallest girl.

"Pile the fire on top!"

Julie smiled. "Not the fire, but more hot coals. That's right." As she worked carefully, Julie told them, "Now you will all be going over to the cooper's shop to see him work for a little while. Then you can come back here, and we'll see how our cake tastes."

As she turned to face them, her long skirt swished about her ankles. She waited, smiling, as the children bounced out the door, chattering and already anxious to see the next attraction. The man stood aside and let them pass, then glanced back toward her.

He smiled for the first time, and a rush of excitement ran through her, followed quickly by regret because he was one of her bosses, then anxiety because she could have done better. What would he scribble on her evaluation form? Would he realize how much it mattered to her?

He straightened suddenly and strode toward her.

"Miss—" He glanced toward her nametag. "Your dress is on fire!"

Julie gasped and jumped away from the hearth, pulling her full skirt around to where she could see the folds. Sure enough, a spark had landed on the hem, and the wool was smoldering, sending up an acrid plume of smoke. The hole grew larger and the fibers at its edges glowed red.

She beat at the fabric with one hand. Before she could think about unfastening the skirt, a cascade of cold water soaked her feet and ankles.

She jumped back. The man was

staring down at the sodden mess he had made by heaving her emergency water bucket on her skirt, the wide floorboards, the hearth, and the Dutch oven.

He winced and looked at her cautiously. "Sorry. I think I drowned your coals."

Julie shook her damp skirt and tried to smile. She hoped she could respond without breaking character. Surely that would help in the evaluation—if anything could help her after catching fire on the job. "It's nothing, sir. There are more embers in the fireplace. I can build it up again."

He nodded uncertainly and glanced toward the doorway. "Well, I... I'm sorry. Perhaps I was a little over-enthusiastic with the water. I hope the children's cake isn't ruined."

"I'll see to it, good sir." She grabbed two pot holders and lifted the Dutch oven off the swimming bed of coals. Carefully she tipped it so the water pooling around the edge of the lid ran off, then she took off the cover. She looked up at him with a relieved smile. "All is well."

"I'm glad."

"I shall fix the baking coals immediately, and there should be no harm done."

He nodded. "Great. I'd better catch up with my class."

"Your class?" She stared at him, baffled. "I thought you were the personnel director here."

"Me? No, I'm the principal at Smith Elementary, Tom Darrow. One of the mothers who was going to help chaperone was ill this morning, so I took her place."

"Oh." Julie bit her lip and looked down at the watery floor. She had broken character, but perhaps it didn't matter.

27

She was sure her cheeks were scarlet, and it wasn't because of the fire. "Be careful, sir. Don't be slipping on the wet floor."

He hesitated, then said softly, "Look, this may be presumptuous, but I've been watching you for the last hour, and—"

She looked up sharply. "Yes?"

"I—well, I wondered if you're—uh—would you be interested in going out with   me?" Julie lowered her gaze, her thoughts in a muddle.

"Sir, I know not of what thou speakest, *going out*. Surely I shall leave the building in a few hours."

"No, I mean a date."

"Date? Why, sir, 'tis the seventh of September, 1690."

"Okay, okay, let me put it this way. Wouldst thou dine with me this evening?" His smile was irresistible.

Julie gathered her soggy skirt and

gave a little curtsy. "I should be delighted."

The End

The Box Social

"What do I have to do?" Sam had resigned himself to attending the fundraiser for the town's youth center. His sister, Greta, was a swimming instructor there, and he knew he couldn't escape helping out.

Sam did feel a bit of responsibility. After all, Greta had allowed him to move in and share her house when he'd move back to his hometown. She probably could find another housemate and charge a higher rent than she did for him. She put up with him working at home too, and his messes. Not that Sam was sloppy, but as a graphic artist he sometimes spread out his work—supplies, references, drafts— until the job was done. She never complained.

"Just come and buy a box lunch," Greta said.

"That's it?"

"Sure. Well, and eat supper with whoever packed it."

"I knew there was a catch." Sam turned back to his computer, scowling. This wasn't a simple fund-raiser. It was a camouflaged social event.

"Oh, Sam, come on, it's for a good cause." Greta was a champion wheedler.

"I know, it's just—"

"Just that Kathleen broke your heart six months ago, and you've determined never to speak to another woman if you can possibly avoid it."

Sam sighed. "My heart isn't broken. Let's just say I'm more cautious now when it comes to females."

"This is for charity, Sam."

"Fine, I'll make a big donation. Just count me out for the box social."

"Honestly," Greta cried. "You are the stubbornest man on earth!"

Sam turned to his keyboard and began typing rapidly, but he hoped Greta wouldn't look too closely at the screen.

"Have you seen the new teacher at the Hillside School?" Greta asked.

"Nope."

"She brought her class to the youth center for games Thursday. She's very nice. And she's making a box lunch for the auction."

"No."

"Sam. Please?"

"Last year you had a walk-a-thon. I raised over fifty dollars for you then. I don't mind walking for charity."

"We wanted to do something different."

"All right, all right, just tell me which box is yours. I'll bid it up to an extravagant price, buy it, and eat supper with my sister."

"No, thanks. I want to meet a nice guy."

Sam snorted.

At the charity fair, Sam knew he was out of place. He wasn't good at striking up conversations with strangers. Greta waved once in a while, but she was busy selling crafts and schmoozing the patrons. He wished he'd managed to show up a minute before the box lunch auction began, but he'd wandered aimlessly among the booths for almost half an hour.

"Hey, Sam!"

He turned and spotted his old friend, Curt Weston.

"Curt. How are things at the fire station?"

"Great," Curt said. "Haven't seen you for a while."

"I've been working on a big project." Sam's comfort zone expanded a little. Having the moral support of a friend was worth a lot at these events.

"So, are you seeing anyone, or are you still mourning Kathleen?"

Sam grimaced. "She didn't die, Curt. She went off to Boston with a theater company."

"Do you hear from her?"

"No, and she doesn't hear from me."

"Mm."

"It was mutual," Sam insisted.

"Sure." Curt didn't sound convinced.

The loudspeaker whined, and a deep voice announced, "The box social auction will begin in five minutes."

"So, are you bidding?" Curt asked.

"Yeah, Greta's making me."

Curt laughed. "Your sister knows how to get things done. What does her box look like? I think I'll bid on it."

"Don't bid against me," Sam warned. Greta had tried to hide her decorated shoebox, but Sam had seen it peeking from a grocery sack on the counter that morning.

"What, you're buying Greta's lunch?" Curt asked.

"That's better than eating with a perfect stranger, don't you think?"

"Twenty minutes with a stranger won't kill you. Say, have you seen the new teacher?"

"Uh-uh."

"She's a knockout. Over there, talking to your sister."

Sam turned skeptically, looking for Greta.

"Her name's Ellen. What do you think?" Curt asked.

"Not bad," Sam conceded. He had an impression of a striking profile, light brown hair in soft, shoulder-length waves, and an earnest expression. Greta laughed, tossing her short blond hair, and when Ellen smiled, Sam revised his appraisal from striking to dazzling.

Curt said, "Wish I knew what *her* box looks like."

Half an hour later, Sam and Curt were standing in a knot of men bidding on the lunches. There were only six left. Curt had bid on two and lost out to other men, but Sam was biding his time, waiting for the box with the pale blue tissue paper and glittery silver bow.

The auctioneer, postmaster Tom Veer, reached for the next box, and Sam came to attention. Blue tissue, silver bow. Greta's box, at last.

"What am I bid on this heavenly creation?" Tom asked.

"Ten dollars," Sam called, and everyone stared at him. They'd been starting out in the two-dollar range.

"Well! Maybe Sam Hodges knows something, fellas." Tom lifted the box to his face and sniffed. "Ah! A hint of cinnamon, I think."

Sam nodded at Curt. Greta had spent hours making apple tarts the night before.

"Eleven dollars," Curt said.

Sam scowled at him. "Twelve!"

"I hear twelve dollars," Tom

announced. "Who'll make it thirteen?"

"Twelve-fifty," came a voice from the other side of the crowd.

Sam whirled in dismay. It was bad enough to have Curt bidding against him. He'd bid so high, now all the men in town wanted that special box.

"Thirteen," Curt said calmly.

"I've got thirteen down front," Tom said with a smile. "Thirteen to firefighter Curt Weston. Who'll go fourteen?"

"Twenty bucks," Sam cried in exasperation.

"Yes!" Tom shouted. In his excitement, he almost dropped the box. "Twenty dollars going once—"

"Twenty-one," Curt called.

Sam's shook his head in disgust. "Why are you doing this to me?"

"She said you have to bid. Did she say you have to win?"

Sam considered that. If he left

without buying a box, Greta would strangle him. He looked over at the side of the platform, where she and a few of her friends were watching. Greta gave a little wave and a smile. Sam was about to wave back when he realized Curt was grinning like a love-struck calf and waving at his sister.

"Twenty-five," Sam yelled.

"Twenty-six," said Curt without missing a beat.

"Thirty!"

Greta and her best friend, Amber, doubled over with laughter.

"Keep it up and I'll kill you," Sam said softly in Curt's ear. "My sister thinks this is a riot."

"So quit bidding."

"No way."

They turned back toward the platform just as Tom brought his gavel down. "Thirty dollars to Sam Hodges."

"Ha!" Sam pulled out his wallet.

Curt's jaw dropped. "I missed it. You distracted me, and I missed it."

"Live and learn."

Sam stepped over to the cashier's table and handed over thirty dollars. Eric, the gymnastics instructor, smiled at him. "Congratulations, Sam. The youth center thanks you, the kids thank you, and I thank you."

"Yeah, yeah. Don't forget my sister."

"What's Greta got to do with it?"

"Everything. I just bought her box."

"No, you didn't."

Sam swallowed hard. "You're kidding, right?"

"No, I think Greta's box is the one they're bidding on now."

Sam swiveled and stared at the box the auctioneer was holding.

"No way. I saw Greta's box this morning. It was not yellow. I know that for a fact."

Eric shrugged and handed him a ticket. "Have fun eating supper with Miss Leeds."

"Who?"

"The new teacher, Ellen Leeds."

"The new—" Sam reached for the ticket. "Right."

He sidled up to Curt again. "Whose box are you bidding on?"

"Uh… how should I know?"

"You set me up."

Curt didn't take his eye off Tom this time. "Sixteen dollars!"

Sam felt tired and foolish. "She switched the boxes with that new teacher after they got here."

Curt laughed. "Greta worries about you. She begged me to help get you out of your melancholy. Besides, it was the only way she would tell me which box was hers."

"You scoundrel."

"Hey, make the most of it."

Sam eyed him narrowly. "You really wanted to eat supper with my sister? That conniving—"

"Twenty-two," Curt yelled.

"What? Twenty-two bucks for Greta's box?"

"You bid thirty on it, or you thought you did."

"Are you done, Curt?" the auctioneer asked, holding his gavel between his hands expectantly.

"What? No. What's the bid?"

"Twenty-four dollars."

"Thirty-one," said Curt, and there were audible groans in the crowd.

"Thirty-one once, twice, sold!" Tom slammed the gavel down.

"Can't you count?" Sam asked.

"Sure, but the highest bidder of the evening gets a romantic, candle-lit table for two in the administrator's office. The rest of you chumps sit on the bleachers. You paid thirty bucks, so I had to go higher than that."

"How come I didn't know this?"

"You were too busy trying to get your sister's box."

"So you outbid me by a dollar just to rub it in."

"No, I did it so I'd get the romantic evening with Greta. She's turned me down three times, but tonight she can't say no."

Curt clapped him on the shoulder and walked over to the cashier's table. Sam took a deep breath, squared his shoulders, and turned.

Greta was standing a yard away with the new teacher.

"Hi," Sam said, eyeing his sister and then his new date. Ellen looked even better up close. Greta just looked smug.

"Sam, I don't believe you've met Ellen Leeds. Ellen, this is my stubborn but talented brother, Sam Hodges."

For a moment, he couldn't breathe. He'd almost missed this. "Hi."

Her smile was breathtaking.

The End

Too Many Michaels

Kelly turned away from the happy scene and slipped into the hallway. It was too much, watching her three sisters reveling in their happiness. There was too much smiling in there, too many diamonds flashing, and too many Michaels.

Her sister Judy had chosen a large hotel's event room for her wedding reception. Kelly was happy for Judy, but she'd had enough for now. She needed a break from the frenzy of relatives, music, and laughter.

"Hello."

She turned and locked eyes with a young man coming out of another large meeting room. Kelly managed a feeble smile. "Hi."

He scanned the poster board pointing guests toward the Kenyon-Lassiter reception and then eyed her blue satin gown. "You belong to the wedding party. I'm a friend of Mike's."

"Which one?"

"The groom."

"Oh."

"My name is—"

"No, don't tell me," Kelly said quickly. "Not unless it's something other than Michael, that is."

His eyebrows shot up. "You have something against men named Michael?"

"Yes."

"Ah." He leaned on a tray stand outside the door from which he'd emerged. "Broken heart?"

"No, it's not that. It's just that the wedding reception down the hall is my sister's, and her new husband's name, as you know, is Michael."

"And he's not worthy of your sister?"

"No, he's great. It's just that…" She felt her face flushing. "It's silly, I suppose, but my family has too many Michaels."

"I'm intrigued."

He steered her toward a settee beneath a window in an alcove, and Kelly sat down, suddenly unsure of herself. But there was one thing she was sure of.

"I could never go out with a guy named Michael. Not now."

His dark eyebrows arched, and she gulped suddenly, as she looked full into his brown eyes and saw that she had the full attention of a rather striking man.

"Do I dare ask why not? Your sister didn't steal him away from you, did she?"

"Oh, no. Not at all. But, you see, I have two more sisters, Claire and Zoey. And Claire is engaged." She stopped and smoothed a wrinkle from the skirt of her bridesmaid's dress.

"Yes?"

"To a very nice guy named... Michael."

He smiled. "I see."

"No, you don't. Because I haven't told you about Zoey. Her date today is her new boyfriend. She just met him a couple of weeks ago at a firefighters' convention, but she's crazy about him. They're both firefighters, see, and his name is—"

"Michael," they said together.

She could laugh then. "My mother is going nuts."

"Any more sisters?"

"No, I'm the last."

"Any brothers named Michael?"

"No. No brothers at all."

"And your father's name?"

"Richard."

He nodded. "I think I'm safe, then."

She waited, almost unable to breathe steadily. He was watching her closely, and she watched back, liking what she saw.

"My name is Blake."

She sighed and closed her eyes for a moment, then extended her hand.

"I'm very pleased to meet you. Kelly Lassiter."

"I'm pleased to meet you, too, Kelly."

She looked over her shoulder. "I suppose I should get back to the reception. I escaped for a few minutes, but..." She hesitated, then plunged in. "I don't suppose you'd like to join the

51

party? Or were you busy with something else?"

Blake grinned. "I'm not busy. I just came out of a business dinner, and I was wondering how I'd kill the evening." As if to support his alibi, several men and a few women came from the same room Blake had.

"You're from out of town?" Kelly asked.

"No, but my boss and I were entertaining some out-of-town clients tonight."

She squinted at him, searching for clues. "What sort of work do you do?"

"I'm a lawyer with Pencott and Price."

"Okay." She'd heard of them. "You aren't... married, are you?"

"No. Thought about it once. She changed her mind about me though."

"So." She studied his square chin and

lifted her gaze to his piercing eyes. "So, if you're not tied up… Would you want to meet the family?"

"I'd love to eyeball all the Michaels. But tell me first why you don't have a date for this event."

Kelly sighed. "I just graduated from my master's program at the state university two weeks ago. MFA. But I came home as single as I was when I started the program two years ago."

"No old friends in the area to catch up with?"

She shook her head. "Not that I'd ask to a wedding on short notice."

"Okay. Let's go brave the receiving line, or whatever they're doing now."

A burst of cheers and applause came from down the hallway.

"They might be cutting the cake," Kelly said.

"I can handle that."

"Or getting ready to dance."

"That too."

"All right, then." She stood and smiled at him.

A straggler came out of the room where the lawyers' dinner had taken place.

"Hey, Mike! You going out tonight?"

Kelly fixed her companion with an accusing gaze. "You said your name was Blake."

"It is." His smile skewed. "All right, Mike is kind of a nickname."

"And all your friends call you Mike."

"Uh, well…" He turned to the other man and said, "Change of plans, Dave. I'll catch you later."

His friend waved and walked toward the exit.

"Be honest," Kelly said, looking her new acquaintance straight in the eyes.

"Do you go by Blake?"

"Sometimes."

"Is Mike, by any chance, your middle name?"

"It's not. I promise."

She let out a breath. "All right then, let's go meet the family."

When they walked into the event room, a song was just ending. Her dad and Judy were leaving the dance floor, as were Mike Kenyon and his mother.

"Dad," Kelly called, and he swung toward her.

"Hey, Kel, where you been?" Her father gave Blake the once-over and turned his attention back to his daughter.

"I just took a little break," Kelly said. "Dad, I'd like you to meet Blake—uh—he's a lawyer with Pencott and Price, and he knows the bridegroom."

"Only slightly," Blake said.

Kelly's dad extended his hand. "Glad

to meet you. I'm Bob Lassiter."

"Blake Michaels."

Kelly's jaw dropped. "*Michaels*?"

He sucked air in through his teeth. "Sorry about that."

Her father looked back and forth between them. "What's going on?"

"Uh, too many Michaels?" Blake shrugged, his face taut.

Her dad threw back his head and laughed. "Unbelievable. Wait until my wife hears this. We'll have to line you guys up for a picture." He swung away to look for her mom.

"I mean it," Blake said soberly. "I'm really sorry, Kelly."

"Sorry that your name is Blake Michaels?"

"I never have been before, but right this moment, yes."

She hauled in a deep breath. "I guess it could have been worse. For instance, your name could be Michael Blake."

"Good point. Let's look on the bright side."

"Yes, Blake, let's do that. Now, cake or dancing?"

"Let's dance."

The End

The View from Here

Being a church usher isn't as simple as it looks. Okay, it's not that complicated; the basics are pretty mundane. Dan, the head usher, briefed the six of us in January, when I was first elected to the position, and it's not too bad, really. You scout out a few seats in the back third for visitors who would feel uncomfortable farther forward, and you have to keep an aisle seat reserved for the Eltons, because of Marilyn's wheelchair.

There are some drawbacks. You

have to wear a suit and tie every week and get there at least twenty minutes early. Of course, you get to meet everyone in the church, and that's a plus.

But there are some subtleties you have to keep in mind if you want to do the job right.

Like never, ever seating Mrs. Goodrow near Mrs. Donahue. And remembering not to seat the trustees where they'll have a good view of the memorial window. It cost twice what they budgeted last year to repair it, and they don't like to be reminded.

Then there are the singles, always a delicate matter when it comes to seating.

Miss Nutter started coming late in January. I noticed her first thing. I couldn't help it. She was gorgeous, but in a quiet, downplayed sort of way. She came in not quite late and looked around uncertainly. The church was nearly full. I stepped up and asked politely if I could help her.

"There's a seat over on the left side, ma'am," I murmured, pointing discreetly.

"Well…" She hesitated, and it struck me that she was looking for someone.

"Or there's another, there on the aisle."

Her face brightened, and I seated her, fifth row from the back, on the right side of the aisle.

When I'd gone back to my post near the door, I glanced at her again. She wasn't looking at the people in her row. No one greeted her. But as she sat there quietly, she seemed to take occasional glances ahead and to her right. I didn't see anyone speak to her before she left, except the pastor.

After church, I checked the visitor's book. Alicia Nutter. She lived in the city. I wondered if she'd come back again. I hoped so, if only so I could see her again. That evening she wasn't there, but I worked my nerve up and asked the pastor about her.

"Miss Nutter?" he asked. "Yes, this morning was her first time here. She's a teacher." That was all I got out of him.

She came back, and I made sure I was the one to seat her. It happened like that for several weeks in a row. I'd look for her each Sunday, making sure I was available when she arrived. She always paused for a moment at the back of the church, before accepting or rejecting the seat I suggested. After seating her, I'd watch her between ushering the stragglers to their seats. It took me a while, but by the middle of February, I was sure. She was watching Mr. Raven.

When she got there the next Sunday, I already had Mr. Raven spotted and had staked out a good seat for her a couple of rows behind him, where she could see him without being observed. Sure enough, she liked that seat.

I began to make a few quiet inquiries about Mr. Raven. He was a widower and had served on the church building committee. He had his own business and was respected and well liked. I guessed he was worthy of Miss Nutter. Maybe.

It went like that for a couple of months. She seemed gratified. We made polite conversation, and she started calling me by my first name, Rick. I felt like I was her personal doorman or something, sort of taking care of her. I liked her, and she seemed to like me, as part of the scenery. We never mentioned Mr. Raven. I just always made sure she had a good view. And she always rewarded me with a smile that made my heart pound.

I started thinking Mr. Raven was

nuts not to turn around and look at her. If he caught the full effect of that smile, he would surely lose his heart immediately. If and when he ever took notice of her, he'd better be good to her, I determined, or he'd have to answer to me.

The fatal day came on Easter Sunday. I'd known it would happen eventually. There were lots of visitors, and not many empty seats by the time Miss Nutter came in. But there was a space in the row beside Mr. Raven.

We stood for an instant together at the back of the auditorium, and I nodded toward the spot in question.

She smiled up at me, and I thought her lip trembled just a bit. We started down the aisle toward the eighth row, and she slipped her hand through my arm. The ladies don't usually do that, but it was kind of nice, and I thought she must be feeling nervous because I was taking her right to where Mr. Raven sat. I walked solemnly, trying to be supportive. If I'd felt we were truly friends, I'd have given her a little pep talk, but we weren't, so I just gave her an encouraging smile.

At the end of the pew I stopped, and she looked up at me from under mile-long eyelashes. "Thank you, Rick," she whispered.

I left her and went back to my post. Dan and I closed the auditorium doors and sat down in our chairs at the back. I could barely see her. She seemed to be looking straight ahead. I never saw her glance at Mr. Raven, all through the special music and the pastor's fine Easter sermon.

Maybe when the service ended, they would speak. She must be full of anticipation, planning what to say to him.

Suddenly it was over, and the organist was playing. Dan and I hopped to open the doors. When I turned around, she was hurrying down the aisle toward us, obviously trying to beat the crowd to the exit. She must have been too nervous to speak to him. I was a little disappointed for her.

When she came even with the door, I caught her eye.

"Have a good Easter, Miss Nutter."

She hesitated just an instant. "Thank you. You too."

On impulse, I walked across the foyer beside her to hold the big front door open for her, trying to work up my courage to broach the subject. "Mr. Raven looks well today," I ventured, as the door swung open.

She looked up at me blankly. "Who?"

I swallowed hard. "Mr. Raven. The man you sat beside."

She shook her head slightly. "I guess

I don't know him."

I stared at her in confusion. I couldn't just let it go. I stepped out into the bright spring sunlight with her. "I thought you did."

"No. Should I?"

I shrugged. "I guess not. Sorry."

She wavered there on the steps, glancing toward the parking lot, then back at me. "So, Rick, is your family having a big dinner today?"

"No. My folks are in Texas. I don't have any family in town. How about you?"

She pulled in a big breath. "Actually, yes, we're having a holiday dinner together. Would you like to join us?"

"Me?" It came out sort of half question and half croak.

She looked away, then back at me, sort of wincing. "It's just my parents and my brother and his wife and me. I just

67

thought—" She broke off helplessly, and I could tell she was embarrassed. The blush made her even more beautiful.

"I'd love to," I said quickly, before she could retract the invitation.

She smiled slowly. "Good. I'm glad."

People were coming out the door and moving around us, so I started walking down the steps with her. It sank in that she'd just asked me to dinner, and that she really wanted to spend the afternoon with me, not Mr. Raven. Maybe she just thought I was lonely and was sorry for me.

I turned to face her on the walkway. "If you're sure you want me to, Miss Nutter."

"Alicia," she murmured. "I'm sure. I—I told my mom I might bring someone home with me, but at the last minute I almost didn't dare to ask you."

I nodded, thinking about that. "Where are you parked? I'll follow you."

"Over there." She nodded toward the far end of the parking lot, but she was looking at me.

I couldn't help it. I crooked my arm just a little toward her, and her hand slipped lightly through it.

As I watched her face, the wattage on that gorgeous smile cranked up to the brilliant level. And it was for me.

The End

Thanksgiving Date

I really didn't expect Steve to show up. I sat on the big rock at the edge of the lake hoping I wouldn't have to wait long in the late November chill. I was in town for a family Thanksgiving gathering and here, on the rock, to keep a date I'd made ten years ago.

A lot had changed in our town in the last decade. If Steve did show up, he'd be surprised when he drove down the main road and saw all the new businesses.

The biggest change was definitely here, on the lake shore. A large tract—the tract that Steve and I had once considered ours—had been sold and developed. The Lakeview Restaurant was a lot nicer than Bunny's Pizza, the only eatery in town at that time, but it was still foreign to me.

I could see the restaurant from the rock and thought it ruined that part of the lake, made it feel public and ordinary. For Steve and me, this had been our secret place.

But we were kids then. We grew up as neighbors and were best friends right up until the beginning of eighth grade, when he moved a thousand miles away.

I knew Steve wouldn't stay in touch. He hated writing letters, and we didn't have our own cell phones then. I knew his parents wouldn't let him use their phones much. It hurt knowing I wouldn't hear from him.

We'd been through a lot together. He was there when I fell off my dad's hay wagon and broke my wrist. And one summer, we learned together how to swim and ride bikes. I tried to console him when he learned his mom had breast cancer. Last time I'd heard, she was beating it, but I hadn't heard for a long time.

Anyway, it was Thanksgiving Day the last time I saw him in person, and Steve and his family were pulling out the next morning. I remembered meeting him here, at the rock.

We'd met here hundreds of times. When we were small, we figured nobody owned that piece of land, so we pretended we owned it—the huge pine trees, the rocky shore, and most of all the big boulder that jutted out into the water.

"What if I never see you again?" I asked him that day.

"I'll visit you."

"You won't."

"I'll see you again, Kara," he promised.

"Oh, yeah? When?" I admit I was pouty that day.

"I don't know. After we're done with school, probably."

"High school or college?"

He broke the scales from a pinecone and tossed them into the water. "College, I guess. When I can afford it."

"That's more than eight years!" I tried to hold back the tears.

"Let's make it ten," he said with decision.

"Ten years?"

"Ten years, for sure. We'll be grownups, and no matter what we're doing or where we are, we'll be here on Thanksgiving in…" He paused. "Two-thousand-twenty-two."

I didn't really believe it would happen—or that the year 2022 would ever really come—but I agreed.

Now there was a nip in the air, and I shivered. Why hadn't I worn gloves? I shoved my hands in my jacket pockets. At the sound of footsteps on the rocks, I looked up. Someone was coming toward me along the shore from the restaurant.

"Steve?" I started to stand up, but then realized it wasn't Steve. Even after ten years, Steve couldn't have changed that much. This guy was tall and broad-shouldered and had sandy-colored hair. Steve's hair was dark, and he'd been a wiry guy, my height in eighth grade.

"Hi." He stood below the rock, looking up at me. "I'm Eric. I own the restaurant, and I saw you sitting out here for the past hour. Are you all right?"

"I'm fine. A little chilly, maybe." I smiled. "My name's Kara."

He nodded.

Suddenly I realized I might be trespassing. "Do you own the rock?" I felt my face redden. "I'm just curious because I came here a lot when I was a kid. Before the restaurant was here."

He smiled. "It's part of the property. I'm thinking of putting picnic tables out here next summer."

I thought about that. Would he get rid of the rock?

"Why don't you come in for a cup of coffee?" Eric asked.

It was tempting, but I might miss Steve. "Thanks, but I'm waiting for someone."

His eyebrows rose, and I realized he was rather attractive. "A Thanksgiving tryst?"

I smiled. "Nothing like that. I'm supposed to meet a friend. Actually, he was my best friend when we were kids.

He moved away, and we made a pact to meet here on Thanksgiving Day 2022, but…"

I looked at Eric to see if he thought I was nuts, but he was watching me intently. His smile was sympathetic but curious.

"The last time we spoke was about five years ago, by phone, and we confirmed this date then." I paused. "Kinda silly, I guess. I don't even know where he lives now or what he does—but knowing Steve, he's probably mountain climber or a cowboy, or something crazy like that."

"What do you do?" Eric asked.

"I'm a freelance writer."

He smiled. "Nice. Work at home?"

"You got it."

"If I didn't love to cook, that's what I'd want to do."

We looked at each other, and I

decided I liked him. And he ran his own business. I got the impression he was dependable and easy to get hold of, not like some people I could name.

"So, do you mind if I stay here a while longer?"

"Stay as long as you like. And if your friend shows up, bring him in for coffee. On the house."

Eric went back to the restaurant, and I settled down to wait again. That guy was interesting. If it weren't for my pact with Steve, I'd have gone inside with him. Instead, I sat there shivering another fifteen minutes.

I was about to call it quits when I heard voices coming through the pine woods. I stood on the rock.

"Kara!"

"Steve! Is it really you?"

"Of course it's me. I told you I'd be here."

I jumped off the rock and into a warm bear hug. He laughed and swung me around.

"This is great! I knew you'd be here. I've been telling Jenny all day you'd wait."

"Jenny?" I craned my neck to look at him.

He stood back, and I saw another figure behind him in the dusk. "Kara, my best friend for thirteen years, this is Jenny, my wife and best friend for the rest of my life."

"Hi... Jenny." I stuck out my hand and she took it. She had knit gloves with leather palms.

"Kara! I've been wanting to meet you. Steve's told me so many funny stories about the two of you as children."

"Yeah, we had a lot of good times together." And apparently Steve still thought of me as a child.

"Get this," Steve said. "Jenny got her degree last May in microbiology."

"Wow. That's impressive." I squinted at Steve. "What did you major in?"

"Astrophysics. But it took me five years. I had to take some time off and work."

I nodded, remembering how tight money had been for his family. "You always wanted to do something space-connected."

"Yeah. And I've got a job. Not with NASA, but in my field."

"That's great."

"How about you?" Steve asked. "The last time we talked, you were second-guessing yourself on your major."

"English." It seemed rather flat.

"Oh, are you teaching?" Jenny asked.

"No. Uh, I'm a writer."

Silence for a moment.

"That's terrific," Steve said. "What do you write?"

"Mostly website content, but I actually sold my first novel in August."

"Fantastic! Hey, listen, Jenny and I have to go pick up some things from her aunt's house. I'm sorry we have to cut this short. Maybe we could get together tomorrow?"

"We're staying over at the Holiday Inn," Jenny said. "Say you'll have lunch with us tomorrow. I know you and Steve have a lot of catching up to do."

"Well... I guess so. Sure."

When they left, after we'd exchanged cell phone numbers, I walked to the restaurant. Jenny was a science lover. She seemed perfect for Steve, and I could tell by the way he looked at her that he was crazy about her.

"Well, well!" Grinning, Eric came to

meet me as I entered the dining room. "So what happened? You didn't bring him in."

"No, he and his wife are taking me to lunch tomorrow."

"Ooh."

"What does that mean?" I asked with a laugh.

"You tell me. Is your heart broken in little tiny pieces?"

"Nope. I'm happy for him."

"I was hoping you'd say that. How about that cup of coffee?"

I followed him through the room, taking note that at least half the tables were full and the wait staff was on their toes.

We sat at a small table near the kitchen, and Eric raised a hand. A young woman was beside us in no time flat.

"Coffee please, Amy." He looked at me. "Or would you rather—"

"Coffee's fine." I rubbed my cold hands together.

"And some Danish pastry, I think." He quirked his eyebrows at me, and I smiled.

She was back in seconds with a full carafe and a tray. She set a plate of pastries in the middle of the table and a mug for each of us.

My mouth watered as I looked at the Danish. "Did you make those?"

"I sure did. My sister's out back in the kitchen right now. She does a lot of the main dishes. I do all the desserts."

When the server had poured our coffee and moved away, I gazed over at Eric. He looked just as good in the soft indoor lighting as he had by moonlight. No, better.

The first words out of my mouth were, "When you build your picnic area, you're not going to get rid of that rock,

83

are you?"

Eric smiled and winked at me. "Never. It seems to be a pretty good meeting place."

The End

That Jenson Boy

"He's a nice young man," Emma insisted, running water into the tea kettle. "He teaches English. You'll like him."

"No, Grandma, I came to visit you, not to meet men. Let's just forget about it." Julie took two cups from the cupboard.

She had carried her suitcase to the guest room and was looking forward to a relaxing week. Every summer she made the visit to Maine, and she always enjoyed it tremendously. It had shocked her a little when she saw how much her grandmother had aged since her last visit. Emma Wright was still active and fiercely independent, but her hair was snowy white all over, and she stooped just a little.

And she was determined to see her granddaughter settled. "Honey, just because you didn't like the dry cleaner last year, or the town clerk the year before…"

"Absolutely not," Julie said firmly. "I have one week to spend here in Saco, and I want to spend it with you. Nobody else."

Emma sighed and set the cream pitcher and sugar bowl beside the bone china cups. "All right, if you say so. I suppose the town clerk was too old for you. I can see that now. But he is nice."

Julie smiled. "Yes, Gram, he's very nice. He's just not for me." She reached for the cookie tin. "Gingersnaps?"

"Of course. I always make gingersnaps when you're coming."

Julie kissed Emma's wrinkled cheek. "We're going to have fun this week. What would you like to do?"

"Well, the grand opening for the new community center is tomorrow. I thought we might take a look. It's got a meeting room and a library and a gymnasium."

"All right." Julie took two linen napkins from a drawer and laid them on the blue and white checked tablecloth. "As long as none of your nice young men friends are expecting to meet us there."

"Oh, no, dear. It was the farthest thing from my mind." Emma glanced out the kitchen window into the backyard. "Oh, I see a baseball out there. That Jenson boy must have lost it over the fence while I was fetching you from the airport. Why don't you just run it next door, dear, while the water heats, and give it back to Billy?"

"Billy?" Julie asked.

"Yes, he's a particular friend of mine." Emma's eyes sparkled. "He mows the lawn for me, and sometimes we share a cookie or two."

"All right." Julie went out the back door and scooped the ball from the neatly-trimmed grass beside the kitchen door. She let herself out the gate onto the driveway. Emma had written several months ago that the Parkers had sold the house next door, and Julie hadn't met the new neighbors. She went to the side door and knocked briskly.

No one came to the door, so after a few seconds she tossed the baseball over the gate into the Jensons' backyard.

The next day, Emma and Julie went to the community center. Plenty of Emma's friends greeted them, and she proudly introduced Julie to them, but no single young men came around for introductions.

"I'm a little tired, dear," Emma said when they got home.

"Would you like a nap?" Julie asked anxiously.

"Perhaps a cup of tea."

"I'll fix it. You sit down." Julie went to the sink and filled the teakettle. "What would you like with it, Gram?"

"A sugar cookie, I think."

Julie put the kettle on and took down the flower-sprigged china cups. "Grandma, I've been wanting to talk to you about something."

"What is it, dear?"

"My company's opening a new branch office in Portland. They've asked me if I want to move up here. I'd be a lot closer to you if I did. I could visit every weekend." She turned to face Emma, hoping to catch her reaction.

"Visit every weekend? You could do better than that! You could live here with me and commute. It would be wonderful!"

"I—are you sure?" The thought had crossed Julie's mind, but she'd wanted it to come from Emma.

"Of course! I do get lonesome sometimes, and, you know, I'm not getting any younger. Your father's been after me to move down there, and I know he and your mother mean well, but I don't want to disrupt their lives."

"I had no idea." Julie was thoughtful.

"Do you really think you might move up here?" Emma's eager hope was childlike.

"I'll give it serious consideration."

Julie glanced out the window. "Oops, the baseball's back."

"Billy's ball?" Emma shook her head. "Would you, dear? And ask him to be more careful."

"At least he doesn't climb over the fence to get it when you're not home," Julie said.

"Oh, he wouldn't do that. He's very polite."

Julie let herself out the back door and picked up the ball. She looked toward the gate, then decided to do it the quick way. She tossed the ball over the fence and turned back toward the door.

Just before she turned the doorknob, there was a thud. The ball had landed on the turf beside her. She caught her breath and bent to retrieve it.

"Billy?" She turned toward the fence. "Billy, is that you? You should be more careful. You might hit my grandmother one of these times."

A man in his thirties stepped up to the board fence on the other side. He was tall enough to look over the high fence that blocked Julie's view of the Jensons' yard. He inspected her as she stood gaping.

"Sorry."

Was that a guilty look in his serious gray eyes? Julie swallowed hard. She had expected a scamp of a boy to respond to her warning, not an unnervingly good-looking man near her age.

"Uh, Mr. Jenson?" she managed.

"Yes." He was curious, a little wary perhaps.

She walked toward the fence, holding out the baseball. "I believe this belongs to your son."

His eyes flared. "My son?"

Julie cast a glance back toward the house, but there was no sign of Emma at the window. "Yes, my grandmother said that Billy must have lost it over the fence earlier, and she—"

The man threw back his head and laughed.

Julie lowered her eyes. "You're Billy, aren't you?"

"Emma Wright is the only one who can call me that and get away with it. I'm Bill Jenson. You've got to be Julie."

She nodded slowly. "She set me up again, didn't she?"

"She's done this before?"

Julie hesitated. "Not exactly like this. She's getting more creative, I think."

His crooked smile set her heart pounding. "She told me about you. Wanted me to come over for supper tonight, but I thought that might be a little…"

"Oh, please," Julie protested. "Not tonight. I need to have a little talk with

Grandma."

He nodded, eyeing her tentatively. "Still, we'd hate to disappoint her, wouldn't we?"

"Oh, that's not a problem," Julie assured him. "I've tried to tell her I can find my own dates."

He laughed again and tossed the ball into the air, catching it easily. "What does she say to that?"

Julie grimaced. "She says she thinks I need a little help." She felt a blush coming on and said quickly, "She doesn't understand how it is nowadays. My job is very demanding, and I don't really have time to socialize much."

He nodded. "Your grandmother says you're an engineer?"

"Well, yes." She took a deep breath. "Look, I'm sorry about this. I'd better get back." She turned away from the fence.

"Hey, wait, Julie."

She stopped and looked back.

"There's a play tonight, at the high school auditorium. *My Fair Lady*. Some of my students are in it. Would you and Emma be my guests?"

"Is this her idea?"

Bill shook his head. "No, it's mine. Look, I can see you're a little leery, but Emma isn't a bad judge of character."

"No," Julie admitted. "She tried to tell me about a friend of hers—an English teacher, I think she said. Coaches Little League."

Bill smiled broadly. "That would be me."

She nodded. "I told her to forget it, but…"

"Having second thoughts?"

"Maybe."

"Great. Shall I come over now and invite Emma to the play?"

"The tea's probably ready," Julie

conceded.

"Fantastic. Any cookies?"

She smiled. "There are always cookies at Grandma's."

"I thought so, but I had no real proof," he said with a grin. He hurried to the gate and was in Grandma's back yard in ten seconds flat. "I'm right behind you, and I can return her ball while I'm there."

Julie stared at him. "*Grandma's* ball?"

"Yeah, she asked me to show her how to pitch last month. Thought it might be good exercise, but I think it was a little too much for her. I was wondering why her ball kept showing up in my yard this week."

"So you just kept tossing it back."

"Right." He shrugged. "I guess she figured sooner or later, one of us would look over the fence."

Julie smiled and realized he was

watching her intently.

"Come on." She opened the kitchen door. Emma sat at the table, smiling as she filled a third teacup.

The End

The Local Section

Violet dived for the local newspaper's vending machine, juggling her purse, her overnight bag, and a handful of coins. If she hurried, she could grab a *Clarion* and still make her train.

As she fumbled for two quarters, a man carrying a soft black briefcase bounded up to the machine. She looked up, and his gaze met hers uncertainly.

"Excuse me," he said, stepping back.

"That's all right." Violet leaned forward and slid her coins into the slot, then opened the cover of the machine, lifting out the day's local newspaper.

"Oh!" She winced and glanced up at the man. "It's the last one."

His eyebrows shot up as he stared past her. "It's all right."

"You can get a New York paper over there." She nodded toward another machine.

"No, I wanted the *Clarion*. It's okay." He turned abruptly.

Violet grimaced and raced after him, toward the platform. "Here, take it."

His long legs had carried him too far ahead in the crowd, and he didn't hear. Violet gave it up and turned toward the ticket booth with a sigh. Her commuter pass had expired, and she hadn't gotten around to buying a new one. She had no time to do a random act of kindness.

Too bad she couldn't have caught him, though. He'd obviously wanted the local paper. Maybe he had a reason as personal as hers. And her mother had probably bought half a dozen copies that morning and would give her a clipping.

She barely made the train. As soon as she boarded she glanced up and down the car, but she didn't see the tall stranger. She sat down and thumbed to the local section of the *Clarion*.

Yes, there it was. She couldn't hold back a huge smile as she examined the picture. It was perfect. She read every word of the text, then stared at the photo again. With a sigh, she turned to the front section and skimmed the headlines, then worked her way through the international news briefs and the obituaries. The memory of the man in the train station kept drifting into her mind. His dark eyes were unforgettably sincere. He'd looked interesting, the type of man she never had time to stop and get to know, but would like to.

They were ten minutes into the trip

when a passenger walking down the aisle paused beside her.

"Well, hello again."

Violet looked up and caught her breath. It was him, the man who wanted the paper, and he was strikingly handsome when he smiled.

"I'm sorry about the paper," she said.

"Don't worry about it."

"Here. I'm done with the front. You take it."

He smiled sheepishly. "Actually, it was the business page I wanted."

"Oh. Which section is it in?"

"Usually the second."

Violet swallowed hard. She turned the pages of the local section slowly. Yes, there it was, on the back of the social page.

"I—I need this section," she began.

He shrugged. "No problem. There's supposed to be a story about my business, and I didn't get a chance to look at it this morning."

Violet hesitated. "Well, here. Take it and read it, but I need the engagements back."

"Engagements?"

"You know. Weddings, engagements." She felt a blush creeping up to her ears.

Comprehension lit his features. "Oh, sure." He reached for the section she had folded neatly into quarters. "Engagements, huh?"

"Right."

He nodded and gave her half a wink. "Thanks. I promise to bring it back soon."

"I'm getting off at Smithville."

"Got it." He disappeared down the aisle.

Violet sighed. The elderly man in the next seat was watching her with amusement. He looked a little like her

Grandpa Littlefield.

"Looks like a good catch," he said with a chortle.

Violet turned away from him. She read all of the comics in the back section, even the serials that she never followed, and then the household hints column.

The minutes ticked by. She began to get nervous. Maybe he'd gotten off with her paper. *Don't be silly,* she told herself. *It's no big deal.* She made herself read the entire car care column and the TV listings for that evening.

The train was leaving the stop before Smithville when he came back.

"Sorry I took so long." There was a twinkle in his deep brown eyes as he handed her the folded paper. "I couldn't resist reading all the engagement announcements."

Violet stared at him, unable to come up with a reply.

"There's a girl who looks a little like you," he said, eyeing Violet's long braid critically, "but her hair's a foot shorter than yours, so unless it's a really old picture, which I doubt, for an engagement announcement..." There was a definite question in his look.

"Oh, it's not me," she said.

"That's a relief." As if to make sure, he gazed pointedly at her left hand. "Not you."

"No." Violet hid her naked fingers under the sports section. "It's my sister."

"Your sister. How wonderful!"

The older man in the next seat barked a laugh. Violet glared at him.

"I had a wild hope that it wasn't your engagement being announced, but after I'd read the page twice, I couldn't quite figure it out."

Violet stared up at him, not sure how to respond, or whether to respond at all.

The train was slowing down, and she reached for her purse.

"My stop."

"Right," the young man said, and he moved down the aisle behind her. Violet felt her cheeks flame scarlet.

When she stepped off the car, she paused to take a deep breath of fresh air. She hated working in the city. Whenever she went back to Smithville, a longing to move back to her hometown tempted her.

"Will you be the maid of honor at the upcoming nuptials?"

She whirled and stared at the young man from the train. "I—yes."

He nodded, smiling. "You must be Miss Fletcher. I'm assuming that Renee Fletcher, of the short hair and large, soulful eyes, is your sister?"

"That's right."

"My name is Jack." He shifted his briefcase and held out his right hand.

She paused, wondering if she was crazy to stand still on a train platform for this come-on. He was carrying a briefcase and wearing a suit—wrinkled, it was true, and the tie was a little flamboyant for her, but she found her caution evaporating. She gripped his hand and laughed.

"Violet. Thanks for returning my paper."

"No problem. So, you live in Smithville?" He glanced down at her overnight bag.

"No, but I grew up here. I'm heading home for the weekend to visit with my folks."

"May I get you a cab?"

"Smithville doesn't have one." She frowned as her caution radar began beeping again. "Do you live around here?"

"No. In Parker."

"That was two stops back."

"Sure enough."

She stared at him and said nothing.

Finally he blinked and grimaced slightly. "Okay, I stayed on the train because…"

"Because you wanted my newspaper?"

He laughed, and Violet found herself laughing, too.

"Listen," Jack said, "I confess it wasn't the paper. It was you. Is someone meeting you?"

"Maybe."

His smile faded. "I'm sorry. I didn't mean to—"

Violet set down her overnight bag and ruffled the pages of the newspaper. Two sections fell to the ground. Jack stooped to pick them up.

She located the social page. "Here. Can't we just rip it in half? You can have your business article, and I can have my sister?"

"Nope. Your sister and my business partner, Terry, are back-to-back."

She turned the page and stared at the photo that was on the other side of Renee and Bill. "You're an efficiency expert."

"Well, yes."

She eyed him cautiously. "Doesn't it seem a bit inefficient to deliberately make yourself miss your stop?"

"It might be. But I teach my clients to spend their time doing the things that are really important, not fritter it away on the mundane. And this seemed really important."

Violet considered that for a moment. She liked him enormously, and it was hard to look away from his expressive brown eyes.

"Keep the paper," he said. "Terry's even more efficient than I am. He probably bought one this morning."

"I'll do that." Violet looked at the photo of Jack and his partner again. "I like the necktie you're wearing in the picture better."

He smiled. "Can I call you? Here's my business card."

Violet picked up her overnight bag, then reached for the card. She unzipped her purse and began to rummage inside it. The newspapers fell again, and Jack scrambled for them as the breeze stirred the pages. "Just grab the local section," Violet cried.

He came back, laughing, holding out the precious page. "The classifieds got away."

"That's okay. It's obvious that one of us is not very efficient." She pulled a card from her purse. "The next train going back to Parker leaves in a minute and a half."

"I can make it."

"You've got the commuter pass, haven't you?"

"What do you think?"

"No question." She pressed her own business card into his hand. "Call me."

"I promise." Jack flashed a brilliant smile, and as he dashed for the train, Violet had no doubt he would follow through.

The End

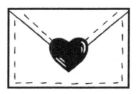

Letters to Kuwait

April 7, 2003
Dear Ned,

Hi! Remember me? I'm Sarah's cousin, Carrie. I was the bridesmaid in emerald green at your wedding. Also the one who spilled punch on Uncle Mack's tux, but we won't talk about that. Sarah wrote me that you've been in Kuwait a month now, and are craving mail, so I offered to pitch in. I'm sending this with some gum, baseball cards, candy, and envelopes.

Tell me if you didn't get everything. Is there anything you need, or anything that would help you pass the off-duty hours?

The klutzy cousin,
Carrie

April 29, 2003
Dear Ned,

That hot, huh? Wish we could send you some cool breezes. Sorry the chocolate melted—I'll know better next time.

I loved the little camels you drew on your note, especially the one driving a Jeep. When you opened this package, you had better have found a small sketch book and some colored pencils. I'll expect full-color doodles next time. Also, here's a pack of UNO cards for your buddy, Matt, and some jellybeans left over from Easter. Anything else you and the other guys in the unit are hankering for?

Carrie

May 15
Dear Ned,
The socks are for your sergeant. The toffee and lip balm are for Greg. The books are for Matt, but make him pass them on when he's done. The rest is for you. Oh, share the Tootsie Rolls. I heard from Sarah, and she sounds a little blue. That's what the phone card is for. Use it well.

Your cousin-in-law,
Carrie

May 26
Dear Ned,

Why not? Send me his address. Love the drawing of the goat at the oasis.

C.

June 11, 2003

Dear Matt,

Hi! I'm Ned's wife's cousin. I guess you know that. When Ned writes to Sarah, he refers to me as She Who Sends Cool Care Packages. Where are you from? It must be hard being away from your family so long. I only met Ned once, at his and Sarah's wedding, but I've heard a lot about him from her, especially since he went overseas. If everything Sarah says is true, he must be a pretty good guy to be camping with in the desert.

I'm glad you're enjoying the cards and books. Anyone who likes both Dickens and Agatha Christie can't be all bad.

This time I'm sending sunscreen, disposable razors, a trivia book and candy. The licorice is for Ned. He didn't specify red or black. Tell him I'll send him another box soon.

Carrie Altman

June 15

Dear Ned,

You're welcome. I sent a box to Matt a few days ago, and now I'm wondering if I was too chummy. If he thinks I'm annoying, please tell me. No, don't. Forget it. Picture of my dog, Monte, riding on the tire swing enclosed.

C.

July 2

Dear Matt,

I enjoyed your letter. What if I said I'm 47? I sent Ned a picture of my Labrador retriever. Will that do? Stay cool.

Carrie

July 2
Ned,

Now what do I do? Matt wants a picture of me, and he's asking how old I am. WHAT DID YOU TELL HIM? Don't say you told him about me ruining Uncle Mack's tux. You wouldn't! Would you?

She Who Sends… you know (Kool-Aid mix and Grisham book enclosed)

July 24
Dear Matt,

I'll think about it. Meanwhile, I'm glad

you appreciated the photo of Monte that Ned shared with you. Here's another. That wad of stuff he's chewing used to be my moccasin.

All right, I'm not 47. How old do you want me to be? Here's a hint: I'm older than Sarah, but younger than her brother, Grant. Maybe Ned can help you solve that one.

I hated *Curtain*, too. She should never have killed Poirot off.

Carrie

Aug. 10

Dear Sarah,

You did WHAT? I don't care what Ned told you. I wasn't looking my best the day of your wedding. The dress was wonderful, but my hair could have been mistaken for a Chore Boy pad. You didn't send him the one of me with frosting on my nose, did you? I'll never forgive you if you did.

Moi

Aug. 17

Dear Matt,

Thank you for your gracious words, but I can't let you think that was a good likeness. That is the ONLY reason I'm sending you this picture. That's me with Monte. My dad took it at the beach last month.

Crossword puzzle book and Tootsie Rolls enclosed (I have to maintain my reputation as a package whiz). Sounds like they are keeping you guys busy. Take care.

Carrie

Aug. 17

Sarah—

I will absolutely kill you!

C.

Aug. 31

Dear Matt,

You are too kind. They say that happens when you spend too much time in the desert—mirages and all that. Sarah was always the pretty one of the family.

I can't believe you never read *The Secret Adversary*. It's one of my favorites. I am sending my rather battered copy. I'm glad so many people liked the books I sent. Enjoy, and pass it on. (The stain on page 53 is just ketchup).

It's hot here, but nothing compared to what you fellows are going through. Those of us back here appreciate what you're doing.

Gotta go—Monte's whining for a walk. He liked your picture, too.

   Carrie

   Sept. 6

   Dear Ned,

That's great news! I thought Sarah would break my eardrums with her screaming when she called to tell me your unit would be heading home soon. One last package here—I hope it reaches you before you pull up stakes. Extra licorice and lip balm included. (Are your teeth black yet? I should have sent toothpaste, too.) And don't give all the lollipops to Matt. I'm sending him his own loot.

   C.

Sept. 7

Dear Matt,

I hope you get the package I sent yesterday. I've given your suggestion a lot of thought, and the answer is yes. Of course, you may not get this if you're already on the move, in which case, I'm sorry I took so much time thinking it over.

Well, anyway, if you want to go to all that trouble, it's the least I can do. If you get this, I'll see you soon, and we'll see what happens.

Carrie (She Who Waits with Great Anticipation and Slight Trepidation)

Oct. 1

Dear Matt,

I'm so glad my last note caught up with you. How long will you be in Germany? Maybe you'd better just plan to call me when you land. Phone number below—guard it with your life. I don't give it to just anyone. Come home safe.

Carrie

October 28, 2003
Dear Ned and Sarah,
I'm so glad you're together again. I was afraid my last note missed Matt, but he called me last week, and we're meeting for dinner tonight. I promised him nothing, and I promise you the same. If it works, fantastic. If not, it was still worthwhile to make a new friend. I don't believe in long letters, so...

Adieu,

Carrie (confetti I saved from the wedding enclosed)

Oct. 30

Dear Ned and Sarah,

Enclosed please find a stupid photo-booth snapshot of me and Pfc. Matthew Smith. Can you tell by the goofy smiles how our date went? Thank you both!

C. (love from M. enclosed)

The End

.

Wandering Irises

"There are irises in the lobby," Melanie said.

Anna looked up from her paperwork. "Someone got flowers?"

"No, it's one of the paintings from the conference room."

"Those are prints, not paintings."

"Well, anyway, it's in the lobby."

"What's it doing there?" Anna asked.

"How should I know? It's where the Picasso was." Melanie disappeared.

Anna rose and walked to the lobby.

There on the wall facing the street door was the large Monet. The vivid irises leaped out at her as she observed the print critically. It was visually arresting, and she was always stirred by it, but it didn't belong there. Modern artists in the lobby, Impressionists in the conference room.

She frowned and went down the hallway. Sure enough, there in the conference room was the Renoir where it should be, between the windows, but over the copier was the Picasso abstract, in shades of blue.

Anna stepped in as close as she could beside the copier and grasped the frame. It was large and unwieldy, but she managed to take it down safely. She held it against her side and hobbled back to the lobby with it.

Down came the Monet. Up went the Picasso.

She stood back. The jumbled figures

of the Picasso always made her feel a
little unsettled. She had chaired the
committee that chose the art for the office
three years ago, during the remodeling.
The Picasso had not been her first choice,
but she had been outvoted.

She took the Monet to the conference
room. Its frame was heavier than the
Picasso's. She was about to give up on
hanging it when Jeff Newton entered the
room. He'd only been with the firm a few
weeks, and Anna had barely spoken to
him yet. Not that she didn't want to, but
as office manager, she tried to maintain a
discreet coolness, even when a man's
presence set her pulse racing.

"Mr. Newton, could you please help
me with this?" She tried not to stare at
him.

"Of course." He set his briefcase on
the table. In a moment, the irises were
back in place.

"The Impressionists liven up the room, don't you think?" she said, reluctant to end the encounter.

He smiled. "Absolutely."

Anna headed back to her desk, unable to forget that quizzical smile. Was he an art lover? Maybe he just thought she was odd. He was handsome enough, but quiet. Office gossip had already told her he was single, but she prided herself on being above an office romance. Professional, that was her byword. It would take a very special man to budge her on that.

She wondered who had moved the prints. One of the partners? Perhaps she had acted too hastily in putting them back.

She pushed the thought aside and immersed herself in her work.

The next morning Anna entered the building at her usual time. She walked briskly into the lobby, then stopped in her tracks.

The irises danced on the opposite wall.

She frowned and went to her cubicle. Although she tried to concentrate on her work, she kept wondering who had moved the Monet.

Later that morning, Melanie brought her a file she'd asked for. "I see the paintings are switched again."

"Prints," Anna snapped.

"Right."

She pushed past Melanie and marched to the conference room. The Picasso mocked her from its perch on the wall behind the copier.

She stood looking at, fuming inwardly. She ought to forget it, but she felt as if someone was deliberately trying to upset her.

Mr. Edwards, the senior partner, poked his head in at the doorway.

"Oh, there you are, Anna. Do you have a free moment?"

"Of course, sir." She hesitated. "Do you know who moved the artworks around?"

He frowned and squinted at the Picasso. "Wasn't that always there?"

"No, sir, it was in the lobby."

"Oh, that's right. Never liked it."

She swallowed hard. "Well, I suppose it doesn't matter."

"Shouldn't think so."

She followed him down the hall. If the big boss didn't care, why should she? But when she came back from lunch, she couldn't stand it. She buttonholed one of

132

the paralegals, and he helped her swap the irises with the abstract once more.

Anna worked late the next day. A large mailing concerning a class action suit had to be ready to go first thing in the morning. She could finish it alone in an hour, and she let the secretaries go at five.

It was a tedious job, and the office emptied as she worked. At last the phones were silent, the footsteps and sounds of closing doors had faded, and she was alone. She finished the job and headed down the hallway to the empty lobby.

As she pushed the door open, she looked instinctively over her shoulder. It was silly, really—

Or not.

Once again, the Picasso had been

replaced with the brilliant irises. How could anyone do it without her knowledge? She had discreetly questioned all the secretaries, and they all denied knowing anything about the art caper. She strode to the wall and hefted the print she had liked so well. It had now become a personal affront.

She carried it as quickly as she could to the conference room, wondering how she would manage to hang it alone.

She stopped in the doorway with a gasp, almost losing her grip on the heavy frame. Jeff Newton was just putting the abstract in place over the copier.

"Are you trying to drive me crazy?" she all but screamed.

He flinched but didn't let go of the Picasso. He tested its weight to be sure it was secure on the hanger, then stepped back, eyed it, and straightened it just a hair. At last he turned to face her, smiling sheepishly.

"I shouldn't have done it, but you're right about those irises. They brighten a whole room. I hope I haven't offended anyone."

Anna clenched her teeth. No one but me, she thought. But she said, "Not at all."

"Don't you think they should greet us and our clients at the door each morning?"

"It's just that this room has Impressionists," she said feebly. "The lobby is modern."

He considered that for a moment. "Well, the whole building is modern, but the lobby is pretty neutral except for the art, don't you think? If you left the Monet out there and brought the Klee and—" He stopped, and Anna realized he was staring at her, his eyes bright. "I'm sorry."

"It's all right."

"Well, whoever picked out the art here has good taste. I haven't had a chance to get anything for my office yet. Who has time to shop? But I've enjoyed what there is, especially the Monet."

Anna looked down at the frame she held against her legs, resting on the carpet. "Maybe you could help me return this to the lobby."

"Are you sure?"

"Yes."

He laughed, and Anna laughed, too, feeling suddenly carefree and optimistic. Perhaps it was time to budge.

The next morning she arrived at the office fifteen minutes early. She smiled at the lovely irises as she crossed the lobby. As she went over the incoming mail, the thought that she would see Jeff soon flitted through her mind. She tried to ignore the slight nervousness that assailed her. At ten after eight, Jeff Newton came to the opening of her cubicle and leaned against the divider, watching her cautiously.

"May I help you?" Anna asked.

"There's a Monet in my office."

"Really?"

"Yes. It's smaller than the one in the lobby. It's more irises, but a different view."

She arched her eyebrows. "You don't say."

He smiled. "The frame is pewter. But, then, you knew that, didn't you?"

"Why should I?"

He shrugged and then grinned as though he couldn't hold it back any longer. "It's absolutely gorgeous."

"You could use another piece, for the

wall behind your desk."

"I don't suppose you'd have an idea on where I might look?"

"Well…" Anna swiveled her chair and looked out the window. "They sell fine prints at the Wilton Gallery. It's open until six. You might find something there."

Jeff stepped forward and leaned on her desk. "I think I need your help in choosing something to complement the irises. Would you be willing to go with me?"

Anna smiled. "I'd love to."

The End

Unlock my Heart

Amber fumbled in her purse as she walked toward the car, holding her package against her side with her elbow.

"Where are my keys? Hey, I love that sweater you bought."

"Me too." Her friend Hailey veered toward the passenger side of the red Toyota and stood waiting as Amber groped fruitlessly in the depths of her handbag.

"They've gotta be here," she moaned.

"Check your pockets."

Amber shoved her hands into one pocket after another with no success. "I didn't give them to you, did I?" Her store bag fell to the ground.

"No, I—Uh-oh. Look." Hailey bent down and pointed inside the car. Amber stooped on her side and stared dolefully at the keys dangling from the ignition.

"Do you have an extra set?" Hailey asked.

Amber stamped her foot. "I let my brother use the car last night, and I didn't get the key back from him."

"We'd better call someone."

"Who? My dad's at work."

"Come on," Hailey said. "We'll go in the store. They probably know someone, and they might even call for us."

"It will cost me a fortune." Glumly, Amber retrieved the bag and followed her friend back inside.

"We usually call the police," the clerk at the service desk said sympathetically. "They won't charge you anything."

"This is humiliating," Amber muttered. She and Hailey trudged back outside.

"Want me to pretend it's my car?" Hailey offered as they waited in the parking lot.

"No, just give me moral support. I feel like an idiot."

"She said 'usually.' I'm sure you're not the first one this has happened to."

"That doesn't make it less mortifying."

A patrol car turned in at the parking lot entrance and rolled slowly toward them. Amber took a deep breath and stepped forward and waved.

"He's cute," Hailey whispered as the uniformed officer climbed out of the car with a tool in his hand.

Amber hissed at her.

"You the one with the keys locked in the car?" he asked.

Amber grimaced. "Do you have to say it so loud?"

He grinned. "I'm Officer Barton. This will just take a minute."

"Thanks. I didn't mean to seem ungrateful."

"That's okay." The breeze ruffled his short auburn hair as he stepped closer.

His smile was reassuring. If she hadn't been so nervous, Amber might have smiled back.

"I'll need to see your driver's license first. Just part of the routine."

"Sure." She rifled her purse again and came up with her identification.

"Okay, Amber Hill. Hey, you live on Maple Street. My sister lives there. Judy Marshall."

"I know Judy." Amber pushed her hair back self-consciously. "She has an adorable little boy."

"Right. I'm Uncle Pete." He stepped up to the window on the driver's side of the car. He was young, but he seemed to know what he was doing.

"No wedding ring," Hailey whispered in Amber's ear. "Oof," she grunted as Amber elbowed her, dropping her package again.

Pete Barton began to whistle softly.

"Beethoven." Hailey smiled.

Amber glared at her. "I have ears."

"Say something."

"You're pushy," Amber whispered back.

Barton swung the door open. "Ta-da! All set."

"Thank you so much." Amber's face felt as if Hailey took a match to it.

"No problem." He nodded with a

grin that included both of them, but his eyes lingered for a moment on Amber.

He looks a little like Joey Marshall, she thought. *Now I know which side the red hair came from.*

He got into the squad car and drove away with a jaunty wave.

"You missed your chance." Hailey's voice was tinged with regret.

"I'm not out shopping for a man. Just because you have a fiancé doesn't mean you have to fix up all your friends." Amber unlocked Hailey's door, and they got in and buckled their seat belts. "I'm starved. Let's get lunch."

"All right. How about that Chinese place on Jefferson Avenue?"

Amber put the car in gear and drove out of the parking lot.

"You should have said something else to him." Hailey pulled her new sweater from her bag.

"Like what?"

"Oh, like how you're *single* and live with your folks just down the block from his sister Judy, something along that line."

"You're ridiculous," Amber said. "It's not my nature to try to start something like that. Besides, cops don't flirt when they're on duty. He was strictly professional."

"Right. He was very somber. You moron!" Hailey hit her playfully. "He liked you!"

"No, he didn't. He thought I was an airhead who shops all day and can't keep track of her car keys."

"He said your name. I'll bet he didn't have to see your driver's license. He just wanted to get your name."

"That's crazy."

"Oh, yeah? He didn't run a check on your plate number to see if we were car

145

thieves. He didn't write down your name or your license number."

"You are way off base."

Hailey shrugged. "He likes classical music. He's perfect for you."

"Would you forget it?" Grudgingly, Amber admitted to herself that she found the dashing police officer attractive. Too bad he'd seen her at her worst. She parked in front of the restaurant and unbuckled quickly. "Come on, it looks crowded. We'll probably have to wait for a table."

She got out of the car and slammed the door as Hailey stood up on the other side. "Oh, no, wait!"

"What?" Hailey swung her door shut.

"No, no, no!" Amber moaned. She rested her arms on the roof of the Toyota and laid her head on her wrist. "I don't believe this."

"What?" Hailey asked again, and

then comprehension dawned on her face. "You didn't."

Amber said nothing, and Hailey stooped to look in the window. The keys hung innocently from the steering column.

"How could you do that? Unbelievable! No, wait. I get it. You want to see Officer Barton again."

Amber scowled. "Leave me alone. Just go get a table."

"I'll ask the hostess to call the cops."

"I'll die if it's him. He already *thinks* I'm stupid. Now he'll know."

Hailey walked around the car and pulled her into a hug. "They'll probably send a fat old sergeant who smokes cigars and has ten kids."

"I don't think they let them get fat," Amber said weakly. "Don't they have to keep fit?"

"All right, a skinny old sergeant

who's ready to retire."

"I will die." Amber sighed.

Hailey took her cell phone from her purse. "Go sit on the bench down there by the mailbox. I'll make the call."

It wasn't five minutes before Amber spotted the patrol car coming down the block.

"Oh, no, that looks like the same car."

Hailey shook her head, smiling. "They all look alike."

Amber's pulse was pounding. "I don't think I can go through this again. Can you handle this for me?"

"Hey, wait!"

But Amber was scurrying toward the bench about twenty yards distant, partly concealed by a mail drop box. She sat down and turned her back to Hailey. Might as well call her mother. That would keep her mind off this disaster. She was pulling up her favorite contacts as the police car came to a stop.

"Well, hello again," Pete Barton said as he walked toward the brunette standing by the bright red Toyota. She was one of the same young women he'd left not fifteen minutes ago.

"Hello," she said brightly. "You're not going to believe this, but my friend was distracted when she got out of the car, and she locked her keys in again."

He chuckled. "I'm willing to bet this is the last time." He carefully worked his tool in at the bottom of the window. "Where is Ms. Hill?"

She leaned toward him conspiratorially. "She's hiding."

His raised his eyebrows. "Hiding?"

"From you. She's too embarrassed to face you again."

He tried to hold back his smile but couldn't. "She didn't do it on purpose, did she?"

"Definitely not. I'm Hailey, by the way. Amber was hoping they'd send another officer and you wouldn't know."

Pete pulled the lock mechanism up and extricated the tool. "Where is she?"

Hailey cocked her head toward a mailbox down the sidewalk. Pete raised his chin and looked at it. A wrought iron bench was anchored just beyond it, and he could see someone sitting in the shelter of the mailbox. She shifted, and he noticed she held something to her ear.

"She's making a phone call?"

"Only in the interest of preserving her dignity."

Pete said hesitantly, "Is she seeing anyone?"

Hailey smiled. "Would you want to take her the keys? I was going to go inside and get us a table." She held out the key ring, a sparkly diamond glittering on her ring finger.

"Thanks." Pete grinned at her.

With a nod, Hailey turned and headed into the restaurant.

Pete walked slowly toward the bench. Amber was talking softly. He walked beyond it on the sidewalk and stood by the other end of the bench.

Amber sneaked a glance at him then turned hastily to face the street. He stood patiently waiting. If only she would smile, she would be beautiful, he thought. He resolved at that moment to make her smile and find out if he was right.

She looked up at him again and said into the receiver, "I've got to go, Mom. I'll be home by three." She hung up slowly and swallowed hard, then pushed to her feet and faced him. "Hi."

"Hi. Your friend is getting a table in the restaurant. Here are your keys."

"Thanks. I—I feel really stupid." She met his gaze for an instant then looked away. "No, the first time I felt stupid. Now I feel utterly worthless."

He laughed. "It's no big deal. In fact, I think this was a good thing."

"How could it be good?" Her strained features said she had serious doubts.

Pete hesitated and almost gave up on coaxing out the smile. "Well, I was wishing I'd talked to you a little longer at the clothing store."

"What about?" Amber asked cautiously. She still looked as if tears would spill over any second from those huge, blue eyes.

Pete looked down at the ground. "I got your name and address, but not your phone number. Could I call you sometime?"

Her smile was everything he'd hoped for.

The End

The Parade

Megan was deliberately avoiding the crush along the sidewalk. The whole town had turned out on Main Street to watch the Memorial Day parade. When it was over, they would surge into the park beyond City Hall for the annual carnival. Her parents' front yard happened to be a prime parade-watching spot, but she didn't press forward like the others.

It wasn't that she didn't like parades. She loved them. Clowns, Boy Scouts, marching bands, the Festival Queen waving from a convertible, and floats created by all the local clubs. And of course, there would be fire trucks. Every town in the region's mutual aid agreement sent a contingent. The firefighters would toss candy and flash their red lights, while blasting the spectators' ears with their sirens.

Megan hung back, remembering other halcyon spring days, when the whole family was together. They'd always had a huge barbecue after the parade, and she and her brothers invited dozens of friends to join them.

Her oldest brother, Jason, was married now and lived five hundred miles away. He and his wife and two children came every year during the week between Christmas and New Year's, and again in the summer.

Megan's parents and her other brother, Nate, still lived in the sprawling

Queen Anne house on Main Street, but Megan had been away to college, then graduate school, and had landed a job in a city two states away. She only got home for a few weekends a year. She hadn't been home for the parade for five years, but she'd thought about it every May. That last parade, so long ago, was one of her most treasured memories.

She had just finished her freshman year of college and was home in time for the holiday weekend. Nate had been studying to become an emergency medical technician and was involved with the town's volunteer fire department that year.

He and his buddy, Jeff, who was three years older and already a paramedic, had drawn the privilege of driving one of the tankers in the parade. When they came even with her parents' home, Nate had stopped the truck right in

157

the middle of the street. Jeff was throwing candy out the window and laughing when their eyes met.

"Meg, right?" he yelled over the screaming sirens.

She'd nodded, grinning.

"Hop in!"

Jeff swung the door to the cab open, and without stopping to think, she climbed up beside him. He kept her laughing down the entire parade route to the park, and let her throw Tootsie Rolls and fireballs to the children that lined the curb.

She had spotted her friend Penny in the crowd at the park, and Nate stopped to let Megan get out and join her friend. He and Jeff took the truck back to the fire station. She'd watched for Jeff all day, but she hadn't seen him again.

Her summer job had kept her out of town, and she hadn't run into him for quite a while. She daydreamed about him during her next year of school and saw him once or twice on school breaks, when he came around to visit Nate. He always had a killer smile for her, but that was it. To him, she was Nate's kid sister.

But that was five years ago. College was behind her. She'd worked at various jobs in the summer, none of them in her home town. Now she was embarked on a promising career.

She knew Jeff was still with the fire department. Did she really want to see him again, after all this time? In her memory, he was perfect. Good looking, witty, fun to be with. Riding in the tanker with him and Nate had made her feel alive and special. If she got a close-up view of him now, she would probably be disappointed.

She knew he wasn't married. Nate and Jeff had kept up their friendship, and over the years Megan had heard snippets about Jeff's life without really trying. Jeff was dating a girl who worked at the hospital; he'd bought an old Mustang and was restoring it; Nate and Jeff had been to fire school together to upgrade their credentials; Jeff had a new girlfriend; the girl had broken it off; and, most recently, Jeff had been promoted.

Megan hadn't wanted to question Nate too closely on this latest trip home. He might get the idea that she'd been pining for Jeff all this time. She hadn't. It was just that every time she thought of home and the promising days of spring, she saw Jeff's tousled blond hair and the glorious grin that warmed her to her toes.

If she saw him today, it might spoil all her fantasies. A lot of things had changed in five years. The fire department was no longer composed of volunteers. The firefighters were paid now, and Jeff was a lieutenant.

She had changed, too, as she matured. She'd had her own plans and disappointments, but the remembered Jeff was a constant. If she didn't see him again, the memory wouldn't change. He would always be friendly and appealing, just out of reach, but someone she would love to know better.

Watching the parade this morning was decidedly dangerous. If Jeff turned out to be less wonderful than she imagined, she would no longer have an ideal to measure other men against.

The color guard marched past, followed by the Festival Queen, the younger sister of one of Megan's classmates. The girl turned from side to side in the car as she waved, steadying her tiara with her free hand. Megan waved back, knowing that if she stayed here on the sidewalk with her parents she wouldn't be able to resist watching the high school band and the floats, and if she did that she'd almost certainly stick around for the antique autos and go-carts.

And if she stayed for them, how could she turn away when the fire trucks rolled by, with her own brother waving from the tanker? And if she saw the gleaming engines, how could she possibly avoid seeing Ladder 3, with Lieutenant Jeff Nye at the wheel?

She'd been home two days and had driven to the grocery store the day before with her mother. Their route necessitated going past the fire station.

"Say, wasn't that Jeff Nye washing the ladder truck?" Her mother craned her neck to look back.

Megan couldn't look without the risk of rear-ending the car in front of her. "Probably sprucing up for the parade. Hey, Mom, look. They finished the new ramp at the post office."

For the rest of the day she'd felt cheated. It was silly. She was twenty-four and still had a school-girl crush on a fireman she'd admired years ago. She should have followed her first instinct and skipped the parade altogether.

She could hear the bass drum thudding up Main Street, and a strain of "American Patrol" wafted to her ears.

"Here comes the band!" Her mother began waving a flag, and her father stepped down off the curb, camera poised, as the uniformed students came into sight down the street.

"Say, Mom, I think I'll go mix up some lemonade for the barbecue. Want me to start the chicken?"

"What? You can't leave now." Her mother waved at the Brownies riding on the Girl Scouts' float and called to them, "You look great! Nice float!"

Megan tried to quell the storm of emotion that welled up in her when the band passed, with the majorettes stepping precisely and the crisp brass notes enveloping them. Maybe she could retreat to the house before the sirens let loose.

Too late. The first wails reached her, even as she tried to decide. She couldn't walk away now.

She stepped up beside her mother, unable to look away from the gleaming engines. Nate's spotless truck crept slowly past them, and one of the rookie firefighters tossed penny candy at them. Megan clapped her hands over her ears as the siren flared to its loudest.

Ladder 3 was next in line, and she eagerly looked into the cab, expecting to see Jeff driving. Instead, he was in the passenger seat, grinning down at her.

"Hey, Meg!"

She smiled in delight. "Hey, Jeff!" He remembered her. She waved, then winced and put her hand back over her ear, feeling slightly ridiculous. He looked better than he had in her girlish daydreams. More mature, of course, but solid and competent, and very happy.

Jeff turned to the driver, and the truck came to a stop right in front of her and her parents. He said something in her direction, but the noise was so loud she couldn't make out a word.

"What?" she screamed.

Suddenly the siren was cut off, and in the lull he yelled, "Hop in, beautiful!"

Megan took her hands from her ears as he threw the cab door open. He stepped part way out onto the sidewalk and extended his hand toward her.

"Great to see you again," he said, and she knew she wouldn't go back to the city without establishing some type of regular contact with him.

Jeff arched his perfect eyebrows at her. "Coming along for the ride?"

Megan smiled and put her hand in his. "Can I throw the candy?"

The End

Special Delivery

Rebecca typed furiously, trying to concentrate on her assignment and forget about last night. James Watson was not worth thinking about, and she was determined to keep her thoughts on business.

It was late afternoon, and she had stuck to her editing job all day, stopping just long enough to eat lunch and put the trash can at the curb for the early morning pickup. In the trash can was every note James had ever written her and every photo she had of him.

The doorbell rang. Rebecca sighed. Working at home had its disadvantages, but she was almost glad for the interruption.

She opened the door to a tall man holding a blue box. On the pocket of his crisp white shirt was *Dan*, embroidered in blue, and above that were a handsome face, a dazzling smile, deep brown eyes, and curly dark hair.

"Rebecca Maxwell?" he asked.

"Yes." Rebecca looked past him toward the delivery van that sat in the driveway. *Dan's Flowers.*

"You're Dan? *The* Dan?"

"Yes."

"You own the florist shop?"

He shrugged. "I do. It started as a partnership with my sister, but she got married and bailed on me." He held out the box.

"What's this?"

"Flowers for you. Someone wants to brighten your day."

"Is there a card?" she asked warily.

Dan held out a small envelope. "Here you go."

Rebecca tore it open. "He makes my blood boil," she choked.

"Sorry," Dan said with half a wince.

"Look at this!" She held the card out to him. "*You're right, I'm an idiot. I'll call you tonight.* Men! They think flowers will fix anything."

"Well, in any case, here's your bouquet."

"I don't want them."

He hesitated. "I'm sorry, but he's paying me to deliver them."

Rebecca sighed. "All right, all right." She took the box and headed down the driveway.

She could feel his eyes on her as she

strode to the trash can. She crushed the box down into the can.

"That bad, huh?"

She glanced up at Dan. He had followed her down the drive.

"No reflection on you or your product," she assured him.

"Bluebird roses," he said mournfully. "A dozen."

"Are they expensive?"

"Very."

"Good." She put the cover on the trash can. "Thank you, Dan. If the customer inquires, you can report that you delivered them."

When she got to the door, she turned back for one last look. He was getting into the van, but he was watching her too. He waved and threw her one last smile. Too bad we couldn't have met under different circumstances, she thought.

The next day, Rebecca had more trouble concentrating than the day before. She had settled things with James when he called, but he wasn't the one who now occupied her thoughts. Her mind kept straying to the florist.

This is stupid, her brain told her. Classic rebound syndrome. But her heart said, You'd had it with James a long time ago. It just took one last, unforgiveable blunder on his part to finish things. She plunged back into editing.

At four o'clock, the doorbell rang.

"Hi." Dan looked slightly apologetic as he held out a florist's box.

"Do you always make the deliveries?"

"No, we have someone, but she was sick yesterday, and—well, today—" He shrugged.

"Well, thanks, but I don't want these."

Dan hesitated.

"Oh, all right," she relented. "I'll take them. The trash can's in here." She leaned toward him for the box.

"Wait." He pulled back slightly. "I, uh, would hate to see you throw these away."

"I'll close the door. You won't have to see."

"You don't understand."

"You're right. I told him last night— again—that it's over. Why he'd want to throw away another—what? Fifty bucks?—I'll never know."

Dan inhaled sharply. "Sixty-nine-ninety-five, but that's not the point."

Rebecca eyed him curiously. "Okay, what is the point?"

"The point is, the customer would

certainly want you to at least read the card before you decide what to do with his gift."

Rebecca arched her eyebrows. "Is it the flowers? You can't stand to see them disposed of?"

"No, not that. I just think you should give this guy a chance."

She stared at him. "Give him a chance? Do you know him?"

Dan looked out toward his van. "Yeah, I know him."

"Well, I gave him many chances. Too many. Trust me, he's an idiot."

"I'm starting to believe that."

"Well, James Watson is history as far as I'm concerned. The next man I get involved with is going to be very different from him."

Dan's eyes flickered. "In what way?"

"He'll be a one-woman man, for starters." She realized her anger had

173

surged into her voice, and she shook her head. "Sorry. Why am I even talking to you about this?"

"Because I'm a sympathetic listener?"

She looked grudgingly into his eyes. "So, how do you know James?"

"I don't know James."

Exasperated, Rebecca sighed. "You just said you did."

"No, I said I know the guy who sent these flowers. Not—not James. His name isn't James."

Rebecca stared at him for three seconds then snatched the envelope that was taped to the top of the box. She turned away from the doorway and opened the card.

I hope you're having a better day today. Is there any chance you would be free for dinner on Friday? Dan

Slowly, she turned around and lifted

her gaze to his.

He smiled sheepishly. "It seemed like a good idea at the time."

She took two steps toward him and reached for the box. He held it out, and she lifted the lid.

"Oh, how lovely." She touched a bird of paradise with one fingertip.

"Well, I saw how you feel about roses."

She laughed. "Actually, I love roses, but... not today."

"So, you would consider dinner on Friday?"

Go slow, Rebecca warned herself, but her heart was pounding in her chest. "Well..."

"I think I'm very different from James."

"Did you see him? Yesterday, I mean, when he ordered the roses."

Dan shook his head. "He didn't come

into the shop. The order was called in."

"Oh." Rebecca took a deep breath. "He took me to the Weathervane the other night. I confronted him about some things, and we had an awful fight. I don't think the management there wants to see me again anytime soon."

Dan smiled. "Have you broken up with anyone at the Manor recently? I made a reservation for seven o'clock."

Rebecca laughed and took the box from his arms. "I'd better get these in water. Come by at six thirty. I'll be ready."

The End

About the author

Susan Page Davis is the author of more than one hundred published novels. She's a two-time winner of the Inspirational Readers' Choice Award and the Will Rogers Medallion, and also a winner of the Carol Award and a finalist in the WILLA Literary Awards. A Maine native, she now lives in Kentucky. If you liked this book, please consider writing a review and posting it on Amazon, Goodreads, or the venue of your choice.

Find Susan at:
Website: https://susanpagedavis.com
BookBub: https://www.bookbub.com/authors/susan-page-davis
Twitter: @SusanPageDavis
Facebook:
https://www.facebook.com/susanpagedavisauthor

Susan's full-length novels you might enjoy:

Mystery and Romantic Suspense:

True Blue Mysteries:
   Blue Plate Special
   Ice Cold Blue
   Persian Blue Puzzle (releases April 2022)
Skirmish Cove Mysteries
   Cliffhanger
   The Plot Thickens (releases November, 2022)
The Maine Justice series:
   The Priority Unit
   Fort Point
   Found Art
   Heartbreaker Hero
   The House Next Door
   The Labor Day Challenge
   Ransom of the Heart
The Saboteur

The Frasier Island Series:
   Frasier Island
   Finding Marie
   Inside Story
Just Cause
You Shouldn't Have
On a Killer's Trail
Hearts in the Crosshairs
What a Picture's Worth
The Mainely Mysteries Series (coauthored
by Susan's daughter, Megan Elaine Davis):
   Homicide at Blue Heron Lake
   Treasure at Blue Heron Lake
   Impostors at Blue Heron Lake
Trail to Justice
Alaska Weddings Series:
   Always Ready
   Fire and Ice
   Polar Opposites
Tearoom Mysteries (from Guideposts,
books written by several authors):
   Tearoom for Two
   Trouble Brewing

Steeped in Secrets
Beneath the Surface
Tea and Promises
Tea Leaves and Legacies

Historical novels:

Homeward Trails Series:
    The Rancher's Legacy
    The Corporal's Codebook
    The Sister's Search (releases July 2022)
The Outlaw Takes a Bride (western)
Counterfeit Captive
Almost Arizona
River Rest (set in 1918)
The Crimson Cipher (set in 1915)
Mrs. Mayberry Meets Her Match
Hearts of Oak Series (Co-authored with
Susan's son James S. Davis, set in the
1850s):
    The Seafaring Women of the Vera B.
    The Scottish Lass

The Ladies' Shooting Club Series (westerns):
    The Sheriff's Surrender
    The Gunsmith's Gallantry
    The Blacksmith's Bravery
Captive Trail (western)
Cowgirl Trail (western)
Hearts in Pursuit (western novella)
Christmas Next Door
Echo Canyon
The Prairie Dreams series (set in the 1850s):
    The Lady's Maid
    Lady Anne's Quest
    A Lady in the Making
Maine Brides series (set in 1720, 1820, and 1895):
    The Prisoner's Wife
    The Castaway's Bride
    The Lumberjack's Lady
Seven Brides for Seven Texans
Seven Brides for Seven Texas Rangers

White Mountain Brides series (set in the 1690's in New Hampshire)
Wyoming Brides series (set in 1850s):
  Protecting Amy
  The Oregon Escort
  Wyoming Hoofbeats
The Island Bride (set in the 1850s)

And many more! **See all of her books** at:

https://susanpagedavis.com

And sign up for Susan's occasional newsletter at:

https://madmimi.com/signups/118177/join

Made in the USA
Monee, IL
05 May 2022

95937880R00105